How We P

by Anita Harper
with pictures by Christine Roche

of the Kids' Book Group

Kestrel Books

People play everywhere.

Some people have a lot of space to play in

and some people don't.

Some people have lots of toys to play with.

Others have only a few.

People often play with anything they find.

Sometimes people play at being other people.

Some people play all the time.

Other people don't have much time to play.

Some people work so that others can have a good time.

Some days people play to win.

Some days they play for fun.

Sometimes games start well

but end badly.

Sometimes people can't play where they want to.

Sometimes people make things to play with.

Sometimes people like to stand and watch.

Some people never stop playing.